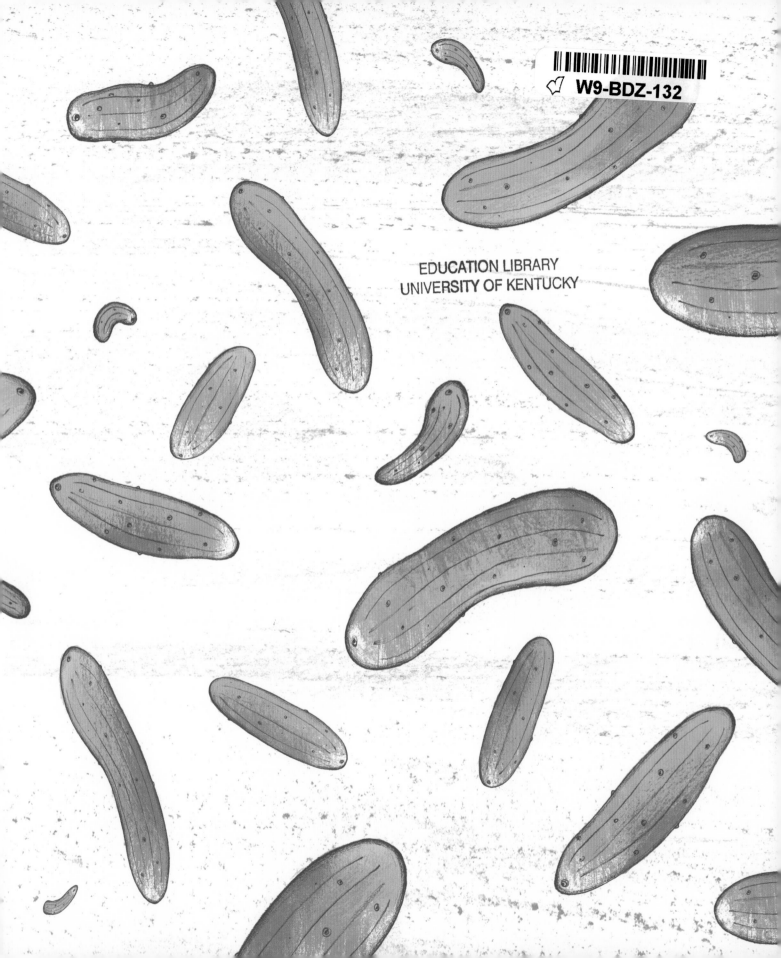

Educ
JE
KUL

Monica Kulling

The Tweedles
Go Online

Pictures by
Marie Lafrance

GROUNDWOOD BOOKS
HOUSE OF ANANSI PRESS
TORONTO   BERKELEY

It was a perfect day for making pickles.
The cucumbers were washed, and the mason jars were
lined up on the counter. Mama was measuring spices
when Gladys Hamm rushed in all aflutter.

"We've got a telephone! We are online!" exclaimed
a delighted Gladys.

"Online?" replied Mama. "What about disease?"

Mama had heard that telephones spread germs.

"Oh, pish posh," replied Gladys. "The telephone is
a marvel."

"I order my groceries by telephone," Gladys
bragged. "I call up my friends right, left and center.
Why, I've already spoken to my sister three times this
morning!"

How extreme, thought Mama.

"Doesn't your ear hurt from all that talking?"
she asked.

All afternoon Mama made pickles and thought about how handy it would be to order groceries by telephone.

At supper Mama made a surprise announcement.

"We are going online! We are getting a telephone."

Frances, or Franny as her friends called her, shouted, "Goody gumdrops!"

Secretly, Franny had wanted a telephone for weeks, months, maybe even a year. She grabbed Mama's hands and together they danced a jig.

Francis, or Frankie as his friends called him, only had eyes for the electric car. He had named it Zippy. "You can't drive a telephone," he said, unimpressed. "I see we are going modern," sighed Papa. "Again." Papa was suspicious of the telephone. People could listen in on your conversations. Papa was a private man, and he wanted to stay that way.

The wooden box was on the wall in the hall. Gladys had promised to call, so the Tweedles were waiting anxiously.

Drriiing! Drriiing!

The bells on the box clanged wildly. The Tweedles startled like frightened rabbits.

"What a racket," said Papa. "Answer it, please, Mama."

"What shall I say?" asked Mama nervously.

But Franny wasn't the least bit nervous. She spoke sweetly into the mouthpiece.

"Hello. Frances Tweedle here."

Mama looked proudly at Papa. "She's so clever, isn't she?"

"Let me talk! Let me talk!" clamored Frankie, grabbing the earpiece.

"Who's this?" he shouted into the mouthpiece.

"Oh, Francis," chided Mama gently, taking the earpiece. "Why can't you be more like Frances?"

"Gladys, hello! You there?" shouted Mama. "Yoo-hoo! Hello?"

Of course Gladys was there. She and Mama talked the evening away. By the time Mama hung up, everyone had gone to bed.

The next day Papa started up the electric car. *I need to make friends with this invention before I try the new one*, he thought.

Frankie was delighted. *"Vroom! Vroom!"* he shouted.

"Drive carefully," warned Franny. She had driven Zippy last month and knew you had to keep your wits about you at the wheel.

"Don't forget to …" began Mama.

Drriiing! Drriiing!

It was the telephone. Mama ran to answer it.

As Papa drove, he kept thinking about Mama's parting words. *Don't forget to … to what?*

In the city, traffic swirled around Papa. Cars, horses and buggies of all kinds were driving every whichaway. Papa was becoming more and more flustered.

"Get a real car!" shouted one driver.

"Get a horse!" shouted another.

"Walk!" shouted someone else.

ALL ITEMS 5¢

Finally, Papa did just that. He parked his car and walked the rest of the way.

At work Papa found a telephone in the lobby.
When Mama got on the line, he asked, "Don't forget
to what?"

"Don't forget to telephone me, of course," said
Mama cheerily. "Isn't it amazing? You are there, miles
away in the city, and I am here and we can talk to
each other."

"It *is* amazing," agreed Papa. "But I have nothing
to say."

That night, after supper, the family sat down to play crokinole. The Tweedles loved board games and this new one was loads of fun. Frankie loved the name.

"Crokinole! Crokinole!" he shouted, racing around the parlor.

Franny took the first turn. She flicked her wooden disc straight into the hole in the center of the board. Franny was a winning crokinole player.

Now it was Mama's turn. She flicked her disc. It hit the wall. *Ping!* Mama was not such a winning crokinole player.

Drriiing! Drriiing!
It was the telephone! Everyone, except Papa, raced
to answer it. Papa sighed and half-heartedly flicked
his disc — so much for crokinole.

It was the middle of the night. Suddenly Papa was wide awake. He could hear mumbling downstairs. Someone was in the house!

Mama was sleeping like a log. Papa picked up her hairbrush to use as a weapon and tiptoed down the stairs.

The whispers grew louder. Papa heard giggling.

Of all things! It was Franny talking on the telephone in the middle of the night!

"What's this about, Frances?" asked Papa.

Franny didn't know. All she knew was that when she was on the telephone, time seemed to slip away.

It was Saturday and quiet. Papa was snoozing. Mama
was baking a cake. Franny's nose was in a book, and
Frankie was in the coach house shining the electric
car until it sparkled like an emerald.

The day was all the more quiet because the
telephone hadn't rung, not even once. Mama and
Papa thought it odd, but they kept quiet about it.

Sunday was also quiet, until the early afternoon.

Bang!Bang!Bang! Gladys Hamm was at the door.

"Your telephone is on the blink!" she yelled. "I've been calling and calling. There's smoke coming from your coach house!"

"Oh no! Zippy!" cried Frankie.

"Oh no! Our horse!" cried Mama and Papa.

"Oh no! I'm sorry," cried Franny. "I disconnected
the bells."
"You did what?!" exclaimed Mama and Papa.

It turned out there wasn't a fire in the coach house. Zippy sparkled. Mercury was munching hay. All was well.

The smoke was coming from behind the Hamms' barn. Mr. Hamm was burning leaves.

"I knew I saw smoke," said Gladys.

"No harm done," said Mama, relieved. "How about some cake?"

"How about a game of crokinole?" asked Franny.

"Crokinole!" shouted Frankie.

Papa flicked his disc. It fell short of the hole.

Mama flicked hers. It landed — *PLOP* — on Gladys's cake.

"No more fiddling with the bells," Mama said.

"My ears were hurting from too much talking," admitted Franny. "But I reconnected the bells."

"Good," replied Mama. "The telephone is our lifeline."

Drriiing! Drriiing!

The Tweedles glanced at one another. No one moved.

Then Frankie shouted, "Crokinole!"

And they kept on playing.

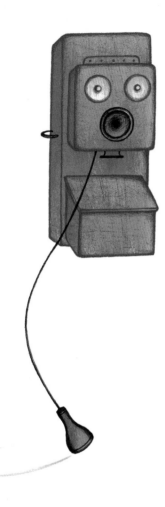

For Patsy Aldana. —MK

To my own papa, who has been online since
1930 and googles today. —ML

Groundwood Books / House of Anansi Press
110 Spadina Avenue, Suite 801, Toronto, Ontario M5V 2K4
or c/o Publishers Group West
1700 Fourth Street, Berkeley, CA 94710

We acknowledge for their financial support of our publishing program the Canada
Council for the Arts, the Government of Canada through the Canada Book Fund
(CBF) and the Ontario Arts Council.

Canada Council   Conseil des Arts
for the Arts   du Canada

ONTARIO ARTS COUNCIL
CONSEIL DES ARTS DE L'ONTARIO
an Ontario government agency
un organisme du gouvernement de l'Ontario

Library and Archives Canada Cataloguing in Publication
Kulling, Monica, author
The Tweedles go online / written by Monica Kulling ; illustrated
by Marie Lafrance.
Issued in print and electronic formats.
ISBN 978-1-55498-353-7 (bound). — ISBN 978-1-55498-354-4 (pdf)
I. Lafrance, Marie, illustrator II. Title.
PS8571.U54T844 2015   jC813'.54   C2014-906746-1
                                                 C2014-906747-X

The illustrations were done in graphite on paper and mixed media collage,
then colored in Photoshop.
Design by Michael Solomon
Printed and bound in Malaysia

FSC
www.fsc.org

MIX
Paper from
responsible sources
FSC® C012700

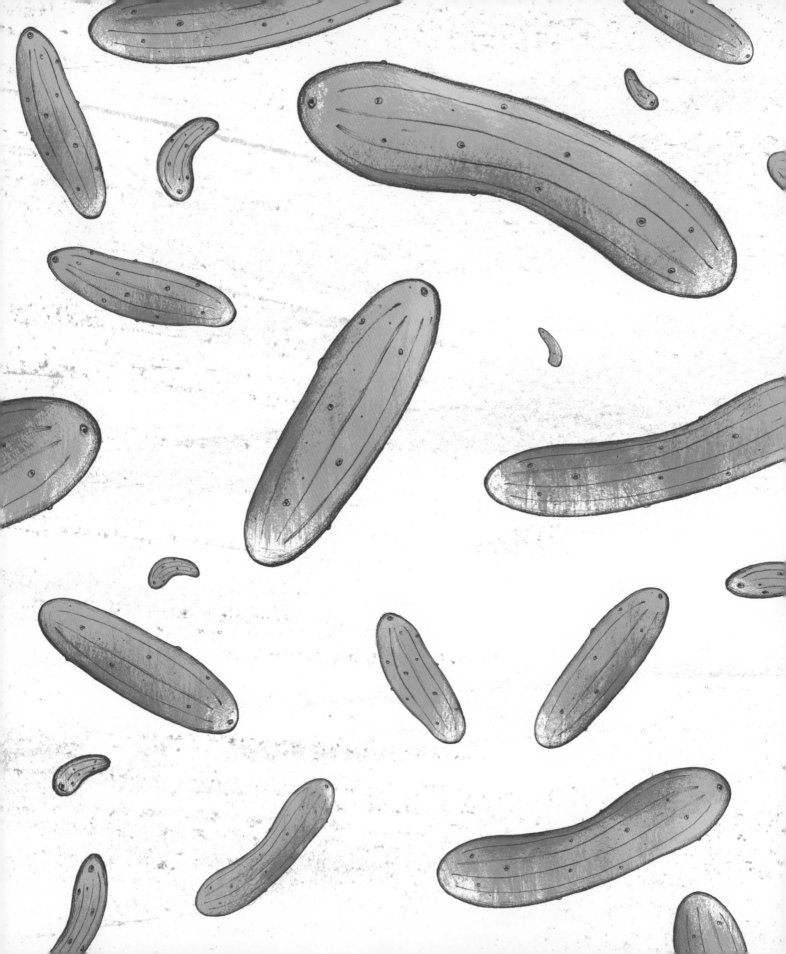